# The Wee Little Woman

## Byron Barton

HarperCollins*Publishers*

The Wee Little Woman. Copyright © 1995 by Byron Barton. Printed in the U.S.A. All rights reserved. Library of Congress Cataloging-in-Publication Data. Barton, Byron. The wee little woman / Byron Barton. p.   cm.  Summary: When a wee little woman milks her wee little cow and leaves the bowl of milk on her wee little table, the situation proves too tempting for a mischievous wee little cat. ISBN 0-06-023387-7. — ISBN 0-06-023388-5 (lib. bdg.)  [1. Cats—Fiction.  2. Milk—Fiction.]  I. Title.  PZ7.B2848We 1995 [E]—dc20  94-18683  CIP  AC  1  2  3  4  5  6  7  8  9  10  ❖  First Edition

12/27/95  B+T  13.89 11.70

There was a wee little woman.

She had a wee little house

and a wee little stool and a wee little chair

and a wee little table and a wee little milk pail

and a wee little cat that said meow

meow

and a wee little cow that said moo.

moo

One day the wee little woman
took the wee little stool
and the wee little milk pail
and went to milk the wee little cow.

She got a wee little milk
from the wee little cow

in the wee little pail.

She took the wee little milk in the wee little pail

**and put it on the wee little table.**

Just then the wee little cat came by,

and he jumped onto the wee little stool and onto

the wee little chair and onto the wee little table

and then he drank up all the wee little milk.
The wee little woman saw the wee little cat,

and she yelled in her loudest wee little voice,

The wee little cat ran away
from the wee little house
and the wee little woman.

**And he ran away for a wee long time.**

After a wee long time passed,
the wee little cat came back
to the wee little house.

Inside he saw the wee little woman
at her wee little table

and on her wee little table
she had a wee little bowl

and in the wee little bowl
there was lots of milk
for a very hungry
little wee
cat.